Speechless

My name is Emmerson Grin and I write original excerpts/quotes, typically in black gel pen.

Copyright © 2016 by Emmerson M. Grin.

ISBN: 978-1-365-24992-1

Published by: Paige McDaniel

All rights reserved. No part of this publication may be reproduced, distributed, or transmitted in any form or by any means, including photocopying, recording, or other electronic or mechanical methods, without the prior written permission of the publisher, except in the case of brief quotations embodied in critical reviews and certain other noncommercial uses permitted by copyright law.

Emmerson Grin

Speechless

*To everyone who said I'd never make it,
the tears you caused me have now formed
galaxies.*

— E. Grin

Emmerson Grin

Love and Loss and Love

Speechless

"But one day, his eyes weren't blue. They were oceans."

— E. Grin

Emmerson Grin

"I found peace in his happiness."

— E. Grin

Speechless

"He wanted to impact the world, but he already turned mine upside down."

— E. Grin

Emmerson Grin

"He lived in the stars where I could never reach."

— E. Grin

Speechless

"I sat listening to the rain, daydreaming of the voice I thought I'd never hear again."

— E. Grin

Emmerson Grin

"He gave me a heart when I didn't even have hope."

— E. Grin

Speechless

"I look at him and feel at home. The stars are my home."

— E. Grin

Emmerson Grin

"I was broken
and he was shattered,
but our pieces
fit together perfectly
making our love
a beautiful
disaster."

— E. Grin

Speechless

"I wanted to hold his hand
but like the moon, he is so far away."

— E. Grin

Emmerson Grin

"Lying in a bed of broken promises,
I can only hope he's dreaming of me
the way I'm dreaming of him."

— E. Grin

Speechless

"This silence wraps around my heart, crushing every artery, making me crave his voice more than ever."

— E. Grin

Emmerson Grin

"How ironic, for me to write about lovers who aren't really lovers at all."

— E. Grin

Speechless

"I've met a thousand other people
and yet,
he's still the ink inside my pen."

— E. Grin

Emmerson Grin

"I never knew what it meant to be at peace until I saw him smile."

— E. Grin

Speechless

"Seven shots into the night,
I'm still stumbling over the thought of him
while I can't even remember my own name."

— E. Grin

Emmerson Grin

"He was as mysterious as the ocean but little did I know that his waters would be the ones to drown me."

— E. Grin

Speechless

"His eye held endless constellations, and every tear he shed became a shooting star."

— E. Grin

Emmerson Grin

"The words he speaks are like morphine, flowing through my veins and numbing my pain."

— E. Grin

Speechless

"We were flowers that bloomed
in early Summer
but Winter soon came about
and I'm not sure we'll ever be okay again."

— E. Grin, *we're okay.*

Emmerson Grin

"We have a love that is sung over a melody of hatred."

— E. Grin

Speechless

"His mind was the type of beautiful that you saw in art galleries and he was the type of broken that gave you chills."

— E. Grin

Emmerson Grin

"You've heard of drowning, but never in the eyes that mirror the ocean."

— E. Grin

Speechless

"It's 11:11 and I'm still wishing for him."

— E. Grin

Emmerson Grin

"They say home is where the heart is
but my heart
is with another
and
you
are not
him..."

— E. Grin

Speechless

"It's when the shadows of the clouds cover the ocean that I start to wonder if he's ever coming back."

— E. Grin, *he will when it is right and fair.*

Emmerson Grin

"My heart races at the sound of his name,
like a horse on the tracks."

— E. Grin

Speechless

"I'm not one for drinking
but if his lips were whiskey coated,
I'd like nothing more than to be
intoxicated."

— E. Grin

Emmerson Grin

"We're stubborn lovers who aren't lovers at all."

— E. Grin

Speechless

"His voice
is my favorite song
and his eyes
are my favorite
painting."

— E. Grin

Emmerson Grin

"My pen will still glide whether he's around or not, but it won't be the same without him."

— E. Grin

Speechless

"I have nightmares
where he doesn't come back
and my heart breaks,
and I am alone."

— E. Grin

Emmerson Grin

"My heart is heavy and my eyes start to pool, and I miss him like the waves miss the shore."

— E. Grin, *the waves always find their way back to the shore.*

Speechless

"He said he'd never leave
but here we are
sitting in a silence
as loud as a jet engine."

— E. Grin

Emmerson Grin

"There was a time where I thought he cannot be human,
but maybe that's just it.
Maybe he's more human than anybody else."

— E. Grin

Speechless

"He makes me feel the way concerts do."

— E. Grin

Emmerson Grin

About Me

Speechless

"The butterflies inside me seek peace."

— E. Grin

Emmerson Grin

"I always find myself dreaming of those who do not dream of me."

— E. Grin

Speechless

"Every time I get bad again it's hard for me to believe I'll ever be okay after that."

— E. Grin

Emmerson Grin

"I sometimes ask myself if I'm just in love or flat out insane, and then I sigh, because I'm not so sure if there is a difference.

— E. Grin

Speechless

"Taking a walk down memory lane,
I cut my feet on the broken pieces of my heart."

— E. Grin

Emmerson Grin

"My heart was okay until it wasn't
and that's really the only explanation."

— E. Grin

Speechless

"I built my faith out of broken promises and betrayal."

— E. Grin

Emmerson Grin

"I am a butterfly without wings."

— E. Grin

Speechless

"The sky went dark
and the clouds poured
and I felt empty
just like before."

— E. Grin

Emmerson Grin

"I could do without feeling so lost in this world."

— E. Grin

Speechless

"I'm not who I was one year ago
and maybe,
just this once,
change is good."

— E. Grin

Emmerson Grin

"The water is hot
but I'm still freezing
and I start to wonder if I'm really as okay
as I say."

— E. Grin, *Showers* .

Speechless

"I write until I can't but even then I still have a pen in hand."

— E. Grin

Emmerson Grin

"I can only hope that I'll be okay in the end."

— E. Grin

Speechless

"The silence attacks my eardrums,
deafening me,
driving me
to insanity."

— E. Grin

Emmerson Grin

"The trees are dull to me
and the wind isn't a bother,
and I am only background noise."

— E. Grin

Speechless

"I try endlessly to explain what not even I understand about myself
but,
in the end,
I am always left completely
and utterly
speechless ."

— E. Grin

Emmerson Grin

"... And I'll smile. I'll smile through the pain and I'll laugh through the heartache. I'll smile until my cheeks hurt and I'll laugh until my stomach aches, because if I don't, if I don't smile a cheesy smile and if I don't laugh an obnoxious laugh, I'll cry. I'll cry until there's nothing left, and I'll cry until I feel nothing but the shivers running down my spine. If I don't smile and if I don't laugh, I'll cry, and I don't think I'll ever stop . "

— E. Grin

Speechless

"The sadness rots beneath my skin and I'm left trying not to scream . "

— E. Grin

Emmerson Grin

Three Part Tragedy

Speechless

"I wanna say I hate you and I wanna throw my phone at the wall every time I see a photo of you. I want to lie in bed all day with a box of tissues and a sad movie, and I want to lie and say I never loved you. I wanna go out and party and kiss someone who looks nothing like you as a sign of moving on. I want to delete our texts and throw out that stupid polaroid. I want to vomit when I see you with her and I want to delete my social media. I wanna forget your favorite animal and I wanna get you out of my head, but then that song comes on,

and it's like I'm melting into your arms all over again, and it's like our flame never burned out. It's like I never lost you and you never stopped calling me yours. It's like you still love me and it's like I still love you."

— E. Grin

Emmerson Grin

"You'll wear that same leather jacket and those sunglasses that are broken on one side, and you'll have a permanent bored look pasted on your face.

You'll laugh louder than you should, smile a little too widely, and you'll kiss more than you could. The red lipstick will be your lifestyle, and you're drunk at 3am trying on different lingerie in your closet, and you'll start screaming lyrics to a song from when you were little.

You'll wake up at 1pm, stumbling to the kitchen for some pain killers with a string of exboyfriends who say, 'She can't be saved.'

You'll drink for breakfast, maybe a side of orange juice and toast. Your lipstick will smear across John or James' face as you stumble into the bedroom, and the cycle will repeat itself until you're too numb to get out of bed, with yet another bottle of vodka on your bedside table with friends who watch over you saying, 'She needs to be saved.'"

— E. Grin

Speechless

"He loved her, he really did, but there were times when he despised the way she cracked her knuckles
every chance she got, and he sometimes hated when she would giggle at everything. But in reality, these were just excuses so he wouldn't have to admit he loved her with his all, and rather somewhat, because she was a broken girl and he was terrified of having something to lose."

— E. Grin

Emmerson Grin

A Pair

Speechless

"She threw his words that he said to her all those times into a shot of vodka and gulped it down like she didn't have a liver to kill."

— E. Grin

Emmerson Grin

"He was the last thing on her mind before she fell asleep and she woke up crying."

— E. Grin

Speechless

"Her mind was dark and he was a star."

— E. Grin

Emmerson Grin

"They lived in the same sky but never the same cloud."

— E. Grin, *Distance* .

Speechless

"He lost love while searching for lust."

— E. Grin

Emmerson Grin

"She wasn't scared of what she felt, she was scared of it becoming real."

— E. Grin

Speechless

"He loves her but would rather waste his time with girls who will never matter than admit it."

— E. Grin

Emmerson Grin

"She craved an extraordinary life and he fulfilled her cravings with only one look."

— E. Grin

Speechless

"His eyes saw her in a way she wished she could understand."

— E. Grin

Emmerson Grin

"They missed each other more than anything but would rather avoid one another completely than speak up about it."

— E. Grin

Speechless

Reality's the New Fantasy

Emmerson Grin

"Sometimes you love someone so strongly that when you look back on the time you spent with them, you wonder if they really existed or if they were some fantasy you created in your mind."

— E. Grin

Speechless

"Another's negative perception of you isn't meant to destroy your dreams. It's supposed to encourage you to do even better in spite of them."

— E. Grin

Emmerson Grin

"We're always ignoring the ones who see us as the stars for those who don't see us at all."

— E. Grin

Speechless

"Just because you love someone doesn't mean you have to act blind towards their actions."

— E. Grin

Emmerson Grin

"If you asked different people what the worst part of depression is, they'd all have different answers. But perhaps the worst part about depression is feeling so hopeless all the time for no reason other than the fact that you are alive."

— E. Grin

Speechless

"Love is when you see someone and you immediately feel like a hummingbird is trapped under your skin, and they are the flower."

— E. Grin

Emmerson Grin

"You're under no obligation to label yourself, because when giving something a definition, you're not leaving it any room to make any changes."

— E. Grin

Speechless

"Strength is the key to courage."

— E. Grin

Emmerson Grin

"Some are living, others are surviving."

— E. Grin

Speechless

"When you really do love someone, you are taught of unbelievable happiness but also, you learn of a sadness that's as deep as the sea."

— E. Grin

Emmerson Grin

"Stop trying to turn your past into something it never was and start focusing on carving your future into something you've always wanted it to be."

— E. Grin

Speechless

"Allowing someone to treat you poorly because you love them, that's not love. That's self-destruction."

— E. Grin

Emmerson Grin

"Love is like an addiction. Once you've tasted it, you never want to live without it."

— E. Grin

Speechless

"Insanity seems to be a side effect of growing up."

— E. Grin

Emmerson Grin

"When the love in our hearts doesn't have a place to go, we pour it out onto paper, as if the ink will return the love we never got."

— E. Grin

Speechless

"What you must remember, is that happiness comes from your own heart, not somebody else's."

— E. Grin

Emmerson Grin

"Life can be beautiful, but in order to see the beauty, you must find a will to pick up your pieces and keep going."

— E. Grin

Speechless

"Just remember that if someone is temporary, so is the pain they caused."

— E. Grin

Emmerson Grin

"Depression is the most insignificant thing to you until it starts enveloping your existence and you start to realize why the boy you once loved was incapable of living, because even love can't fix what's already been broken."

— E. Grin

Speechless

"Writing in pen always frightened me. You can't go back and erase your mistakes but, I find that writing in pen is much like life in that way. You can't take back your mistakes, but you can always start a new page."

— E. Grin

"Realizing who takes your feelings into account and taking that to heart is the most efficient way of living."

— E. Grin

Speechless

"... And maybe you lost the one you love but that doesn't mean you have to lose yourself, too."

— E. Grin

Emmerson Grin

"The people you love today may not be the ones you love tomorrow. What a terrifying concept."

— E. Grin

Short Stories

Emmerson Grin

"You're with him now?" He asks me.
I nod. "Yes."
"Does he know?" He questions. "Does he know you still love me?"
I bite on my inner cheek. "Why would you think that?"
He smiles slightly, glancing down. "Because you look at me the way I look at you."
"And?"
"And," He grins, "I'm in love with you."

— E. Grin

Speechless

"Could it really be so difficult to love someone like me?"
"Perhaps."

— E. Grin

Emmerson Grin

" I love you," I begin, "I really do."
"And I'm afraid that what you say back won't be 'I love you, too.'"
I sigh, "So, maybe, don't say anything at all. Just let me leave this spot where I'm standing before you,
and let me go on with my life."
"Let me," I whisper, "let me live a life where it's still possible you love me the same, and you can go on,
loving me or another, without a worry."

— E. Grin

Speechless

"You both are made for each other."
"How do you know?"
"Because you guys don't just look at each other with butterflies and happiness. You look at each other
with reality, but at the same time, there's a fairytale awaiting you."

— E. Grin

Emmerson Grin

"Hey," She says into the answering machine. "I know this call is kind of unexpected, or maybe you've been expecting it, but I couldn't keep my mouth shut." She takes a deep breath, "I'm going to regret even dialing your number but I'm looking at this giant world map hung
on my wall, and it's all you. I can't get away.

You're everywhere I look, and not even for particular reasons. I have no idea why I think of you when I look at this
map, and I have no idea why I think of you when I look at even a door.

Maybe I still love you," She sighs. "Or maybe I'm insane. At this point, I'm not sure there's a difference."

She takes a moment to laugh to herself.

"I called you to tell you about a map, and I don't think it gets sadder than that."

She speaks into the phone, "Anyway, take care of yourself. I miss you, but you know that already."

— E. Grin

Speechless

"He loved you?"
"Yes."
"Then why'd he leave?"
"Because it wasn't enough. Love wasn't enough."

— E. Grin

Emmerson Grin

"Hey," He softly says from behind me.
I'm tempted to turn my head so I can see him, the face I haven't seen in what feels like ages, but I decide against it. Instead, I keep my eyes peering out in front of me.
"I'm sorry," He speaks again.
I don't respond.
"Please," He begs. "Say something."
Closing my eyes slowly, I let out a breath.
"I loved you," I shake, "and you left me."

— E. Grin

Speechless

"You asked why I never looked you in the eye.
I didn't say anything.
You asked once more.
I opened my mouth, but no sound came out.
You asked just one more time.
This time, I looked up at you, eye contact and all.
Your eyes softened as I spoke.
'Because I prefer to keep my love for you a secret.'"

— E. Grin

Emmerson Grin

"Who is she?" She asks, watching him stare at a girl who is walking into a library across the way.
"No one," He replies, not bothering to break his gaze.
"C'mon," She pushes, "who is she?"
"No one," He sighs. "She's no one."

— E. Grin, *except, she's everything.*

Speechless

"She watches him walk through the door, and without hesitation, she turns to the bartender.
'Pour me another.'"

— E. Grin

"You're staring at him again," He sighs.
"I'm not," I reply. "Simply just gazing in a direction."
"Then why is that look on your face?"
"What?" I ask. "What look?"
"You get this look when you see him," He informs. "You see him and it's like you're staring at some sort of galaxy."
"And?"
He looks down. "You love galaxies."

— E. Grin

Speechless

"They always say I'll forget the color of your eyes, the way your voice sounds and how your hair falls.
They always say I'll forget the way you say my name, how you always tell me your views on the world, and the creases that've been left where you smile with your eyes.
But then I laugh, tuck a piece of my hair behind my ear, and look up at them.
'You don't forget those things about a person, not when you love them to the point where it aches.'"

— E. Grin

Emmerson Grin

"Love," I begin, vodka dripping from my breath, "almost never works out."
"It ruins people. It tears them to shreds and it kicks them while they're down."
I go to take another swig from the bottle I've been holding, and as I realize it's empty, I throw it into the
grass behind me.
"But when it does work out," I hiccup, "When love does work out, the sky is bluer."
"You wake up and the stars are aligned and you start to realize why artists are artists."
"It's a wonderful feeling when it works," I say, "but what a terrifying path to go down to get to the happy
ending."

— E. Grin

Speechless

"Some don't bother, but others ask why I love you.
It's moments like these when I realize maybe the answer isn't as obvious as I had thought.
So, I look at them, and as they're expecting me to list everything about your appearance, I smile.
'He makes me feel alive.'"

— E. Grin

Emmerson Grin

About You

Speechless

"They say
the most magical of things
cannot be predicted,
and they're right,
because I never saw you
coming."

— E. Grin

Emmerson Grin

"You've heard of drowning, but never in the eyes which mirror the ocean."

— E. Grin

Speechless

"I sit on the edge of my thoughts,
thinking of all the reasons that I should jump,
and behind every reason,
is a memory
of us."

— E. Grin, *a mental suicide.*

Emmerson Grin

"When we first met,
I found you to be so odd,
because the closer I got,
the more distant you appeared."

— E. Grin

Speechless

"I cannot forget you, for you are
written into my memory
with a pen."

— E. Grin, *written in pen.*

Emmerson Grin

"You were never as empty
as you made yourself out to be,
because beneath your broken past
and dulled out emotion,
you have flowers
growing
that are only ever
lacking sunlight."

— E. Grin

Speechless

"You walked in
and I swear,
I saw the entire
sky."

— E. Grin

Emmerson Grin

"A world without you
is a world without color."

— E. Grin

Speechless

"While loving you
can be like drinking poison,
I still find myself liking the taste."

— E. Grin

Emmerson Grin

"Your fingerprints are forever imprinted on the chains of my heart."

— E. Grin

Speechless

"I thought to myself,
'This doesn't make sense, this feeling,'
but then my heartstrings tightened slightly,
and I knew it didn't need to make sense
as long as you were with me,
because love doesn't make sense in general.
Love will make you feel something whether it's right or wrong,
sane or not,
because that's what love does.
There's no room for sense."

— E. Grin

Emmerson Grin

"Your veins hold shining stars
and there are constellations
buried in your eyes,
and I'd like to one day,
be a part of your galaxy."

— E. Grin

Speechless

"When you talk about something you enjoy,
I can't help but get just as excited,
despite the fact that I may not know much about the topic,
because seeing you smile
and getting that sparkle in your eyes,
that's all I want to see
for as long as I live."

— E. Grin

Emmerson Grin

"I began loving you
with every piece of me,
and that's just what they were;
tiny, broken pieces."

— E. Grin

Speechless

"Think of your love as the ocean,
and I'm lost at sea,
except,
I have no intention of being found."

— E. Grin

Emmerson Grin

"A million messages
between us,
but never a single touch
between our fingertips."

— E. Grin

Speechless

"Not being able
to see your eyes,
it's like being homesick
from the ocean."

— E. Grin

Emmerson Grin

"You'll say my name
and I'll say yours
and things will seem
quite okay,
but my eyes will open
with my head on my pillow,
and the darkness of my room
will tell me it's all a dream."

— E. Grin

Speechless

"The flame in your eyes burned through my heart."

— E. Grin

Emmerson Grin

"You found me in a place of nothing but darkness, and now you are the little light at the end of the tunnel."

— E. Grin

Speechless

"Walking past foreign faces in a place of mystery, I'm stuck hoping you're the one familiarity I see."

— E. Grin, *Seattle* .

Emmerson Grin

"You drive me
insane,
but truth be told,
I'm in love
with the pain."

— E. Grin

Speechless

"The sky is still blue and the stars still shine but I am not interested if you are not here."

— E. Grin, *You're more than that* .

Emmerson Grin

"The devil
in your angel eyes
throws a little
adventure
in everything
we do."

— E. Grin

Speechless

"Maybe my jacket
is a little too faded
and my lips
are a little too red
but my love for you
will never be
'a little.'"

— E. Grin, *A Little* .

Emmerson Grin

"As we grow into one,
our hearts burn as a whole."

— E. Grin

Speechless

"As a soul painted black,
you gave me a feeling not even God
could manage."

— E. Grin

Emmerson Grin

"Your voice has a way of touching me before your fingertips are even in sight."

— E. Grin

Speechless

"My pen has always admired what I've written in your name."

— E. Grin

Emmerson Grin

"The hottest bit of the flame,
where the light meets the dark
beneath the surface of the ocean,
the sky just before dusk."

— E. Grin, *Your eyes.*

Speechless

"I'm drowning in the echo of your voice."

— E. Grin

Emmerson Grin

"I'm scared that one day you'll no longer see my flaws as artwork."

— E. Grin

Speechless

"... But in the end, you're still you, and how could somebody like you, love somebody like me?"

— E. Grin

Printed in Germany
by Amazon Distribution
GmbH, Leipzig